The Robot & The Ballerina

By Amanda Woods

Published by Mindstir Media LLC
45 Lafayette Rd. Suite 181 | North Hampton, NH 03862 | USA
1.800.767.0531 | www.mindstirmedia.com

Printed in the United States of America
ISBN-13: 978-0-9986975-9-8
Library of Congress Control Number: 2017904892

Work hard and dream big!
Thank you for your support!
Amanda Woock

MINDSTIR MEDIA

Belle Ballerina woke up early one day,
Searching and looking for something to do or play.

She twirled about the house, in this room and that.
Then she came upon a box in the kitchen, left in the trash.

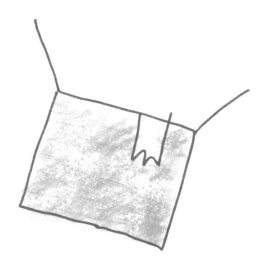

It was just her height, with a scuff here and there.
She had some ideas, for the box was so bare.

She dove in her craft nook to find buttons and glue.
She made quite a mess, but she knew just what to do.

Carl, she named him. A robot painted red.

Then all of a sudden Mom came downstairs right out of her bed.

"What is this mess?" Mom said. "You better clean it up now!"

Then all of a sudden Carl stood up and took a bow.

"My beautiful Belle, listen to your mother,
Let's quickly clean up, don't wake up the others."

We will go on adventures to the moon and in space.
Let's explore the stars and enjoy this miraculous place.

Maybe we'll see aliens or even a rocket ship or two.
There's so much to see we won't run out of things to
do.

After a while we should head back to earth next,
Swimming with the fish is probably best.

Be careful not to get in the mouth of a whale,
Let's not end up in his stomach, we just want a ride on
his tail!

After our ride we will be wet and cold.
Where can we go that feels warm like a stove?

That's it, I got it! I know where to go,
It has rock and lava, it's a volcano!

We'll need special shoes to walk on this mountain,
Because this is the world's hottest rock fountain!

Be careful not to get too close to the top,
I've seen the volcano wake up and pop!

Quick! Time to move on into the jungle deep!
Don't make much noise, let the dangerous animals sleep.

Won't it be fun to climb up that coconut tree?
Wait, did you hear that? We should probably go, don't you agree?

Then Mom said, "Belle, Belle! Wake up, are you dreaming? There was a lot of laughing or maybe some screaming?"

"No, Mom, don't worry it was just me and Carl playing." Then Mom said: "That run down old box is Carl? Is that what you're saying?"

"Yes, Mom, he's a robot that takes me anywhere I want to go.
There is so much of the world he wants to show."

Mom said: "You can go on the moon or the ocean for that matter,
But Carl can take you to clean up, you left the kitchen in a tatter."

"Carl, come on, we have a lot of cleaning up to do Carl?...You're not moving. What happened to you?"

Carl was nowhere to be found -- just an old box with a stoop.
Even his arms and button eyes started to droop.

Slowly she picked up her mess piece by piece.
She hoped that tonight Carl would return in her dreams.

Next time you see that old box on the floor,
You never know what kind of adventure you're in for.

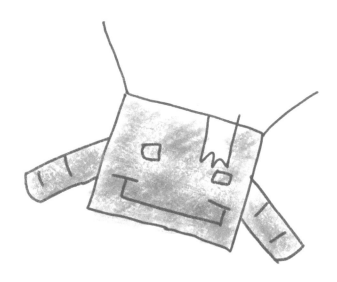

CPSIA information can be obtained at www.ICGtesting.com
Printed in the USA
BVIW12n1703120617
486472BV00002B/6